A Little M[...]
of Promises *for:*

. . . .

First published in Great Britain in 2018 by Hodder & Stoughton

An Hachette UK company

1

A CIP catalogue record for this title is available from the British Library

ISBN 978 1 473 69175 9
eBook ISBN 978 1 473 69176 6

Set in Baskerville by Anna Woodbine, thewoodbineworkshop.co.uk
Printed and bound in Italy by Lego S.p.A.

Hodder & Stoughton policy is to use papers that are natural, renewable and recyclable
products and made from wood grown in sustainable forests. The logging and
manufacturing processes are expected to conform to the environmental regulations of
the country of origin.

Hodder & Stoughton Ltd
Carmelite House
50 Victoria Embankment
London EC4Y 0DZ

www.hodderfaith.com

Dear Parents

I have called these books Little Moments *(not* Vast Hours*!)*
because I want them to be just that. A moment to pause in you and
your child's busy day. A moment to step away from the hustle and
bustle of life. A moment simply to be still.

The Bible is full of the most amazing stories, written down by many
authors over hundreds of years, all of them inspired to share the story
of this wonderful God and his amazing love for his children.
The words in this book are not literal translations – they are inspired
by verses and passages that I love.

My hope for all my readers, big and small, is that the
words and pictures will connect you to the true heart of God
and that the truth of who God is and how much
God loves you will nestle deep in your heart.

Jenny

Hold God's promises in your heart

and in your mind.

Let them remind you of
God's faithfulness and love.

Deuteronomy 11:18

God has written

y o u r   n a m e

on his hand.

Isaiah 49:16

God leans

over

heaven's

walls

to get a closer look at

his *beloved* children.

Psalm 14:2

Throw off fear
and run *into*
God's arms of *love*.

1 John 4:18

God's light shines
in the **darkness**
and will never
go out.

John 1:5

There's no need to hide,

God knows your

every heartbeat

and loves you as you are.

Psalm 139:1-10

God's *banner over me*
is one
of love.

God holds onto me

with safe hands.

John 10:28

God watches over those who have no father.

Deuteronomy 10:18

Sing for joy,
for you are covered
by love.

God's love walks with me,

every moment of every day,

never leaving my side.

Psalm 23:6

I love being in God's house,

where I can rest in the

warmth

of God's love.

S t r e t c h
out your hands
and carry each
other's burdens.

Galatians 6:2

Nothing can stand

between me and

the

love

of

God.

Romans 8:39

Treat your friend
with patience and be
gentle when they
make mistakes.

Even the ocean's
waves cannot wash
love away.

Song of Solomon 8:7

Don't just love
with words but also in
your deeds.

1 John 3:18

God does not rush

into anger,

but has

words of

love *and*

faithfulness.

Psalm 86:15

Hatred creates a whirlwind of problems

but love covers everything
in warmth, bringing
stillness to your heart.

Proverbs 10:12

Love

displays

p a t i e n c e.

1 Corinthians 13:4

In the morning
I will wake up to
your unfailing
l o v e .

Psalm 143:8

Show your love
to your friends
by giving
them
centre
stage.

Romans 12:10

Offer your neighbour
a gift of love,
one that you
would like to receive.

Mark 12:31

If the words I speak

have no love

in them

then I will sound
like a tuneless
noise.

1 Corinthians 13:1

I began to slip
but God's love held
me tight.

Psalm 94:18

Did you know
that the stranger you
are kind to might
just be an
angel?

Hebrews 13:1-2

Be ready to catch

your friend

if they f_a_l_l.

Ecclesiastes 4:9-10

*Tuck yourself
into God's*
love.

John 15:9